Disney · PIXAR

Cars 2

Adapted by **Chase Wheeler**

Illustrated by **Studio IBOIX**

Designed by **Tony Fejeran**

 A GOLDEN BOOK · NEW YORK

Materials and characters from the movie *Cars 2*. Copyright © 2011 Disney/Pixar. Disney/Pixar elements © Disney/Pixar, not including underlying vehicles owned by third parties. Pacer and Gremlin are trademarks of Chrysler LLC; Jeep® and the Jeep® grille design are registered trademarks of Chrysler LLC; Maserati logos and model designations are trademarks of Maserati S.p.A. and are used under license; Mercury is a registered trademark of Ford Motor Company; Porsche is a trademark of Porsche; Sarge's rank insignia design used with the approval of the U.S. Army; Volkswagen trademarks, design patents and copyrights are used with the approval of the owner, Volkswagen AG; Bentley is a trademark of Bentley Motors Limited; FIAT, Alfa Romeo, and Topolino are trademarks of FIAT S.p.A.; Corvette and Chevrolet Impala are trademarks of General Motors. Background inspired by the Cadillac Ranch by Ant Farm (Lord, Michels and Marquez) © 1974. Published in the United States by Golden Books, an imprint of Random House Children's Books, a division of Random House, Inc., 1745 Broadway, New York, NY 10019, and in Canada by Random House of Canada Limited, Toronto, in conjunction with Disney Enterprises, Inc. Golden Books, A Golden Book, A Little Golden Book, the G colophon, and the distinctive gold spine are registered trademarks of Random House, Inc.

www.randomhouse.com/kids

ISBN: 978-0-7364-2781-4

Printed in the United States of America

20 19 18 17 16 15 14 13

Lightning McQueen was ready for **action**. He was going to a big race to prove that he was the fastest car in the world! His best friend, Mater, and his other pals from Radiator Springs—Luigi, Guido, Sarge, and Fillmore—were all coming along as his pit crew.

Lightning was going to compete in three races held in three different places:

Tokyo, Japan

Porto Corsa, Italy

and **London, England**.

Cars from all over the **world** would be racing!

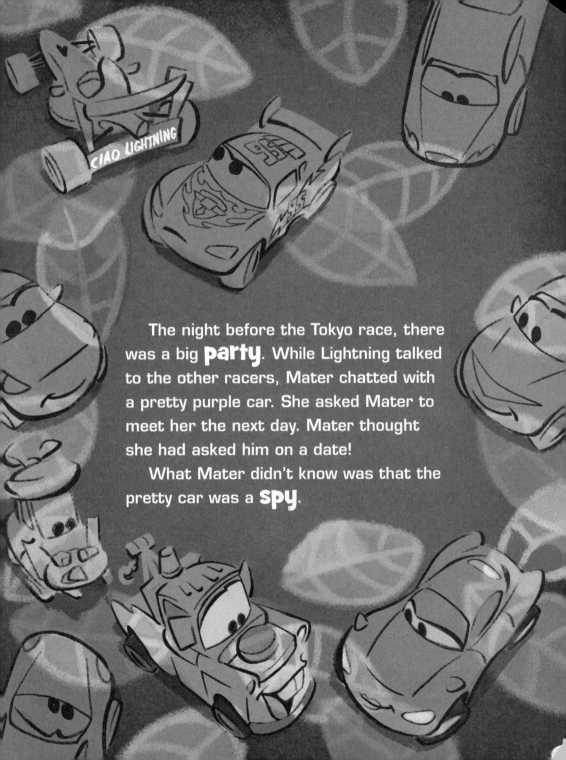

The night before the Tokyo race, there was a big **party**. While Lightning talked to the other racers, Mater chatted with a pretty purple car. She asked Mater to meet her the next day. Mater thought she had asked him on a date!

What Mater didn't know was that the pretty car was a **spy**.

The next day, the first race began. **VROOM**! Lightning and the other race cars zoomed around the track.

Suddenly . . .
BLAM! KABAM! BANG!
Two race cars caught
FIRE!

Lightning didn't see the explosions. He was already pulling into the lead.

Just then, Lightning heard Mater giving
him instructions over his headset:

"RIGHT!"

"LEFT!"

"RIGHT!"

Lightning swerved around the track,
trying to follow the crazy commands.
Little did he know Mater wasn't
even watching the race! Mater had
gone to look for the pretty purple car.
Lightning was overhearing Mater
talking to himself!

As Lightning **zigzagged** around the track, an Italian car named Francesco sped past him— and won the race!

Lightning was upset. "You made me lose!" he told Mater angrily. "I never should have brought you."

Mater didn't want to cause any more **trouble** for Lightning. The next day, he left a note saying he was going back to Radiator Springs.

But Mater never made it home. At the airport, two cars started to **chase** him.

Another car **saved** Mater just in time and led him onto the runway, where a jet was waiting!

Guess who was on the jet? "My date!" Mater exclaimed.

The pretty purple car's name was Holley. Her partner's name was Finn. They were both **spies**. They thought Mater was a spy, too. They wanted his help on a **top-secret** mission.

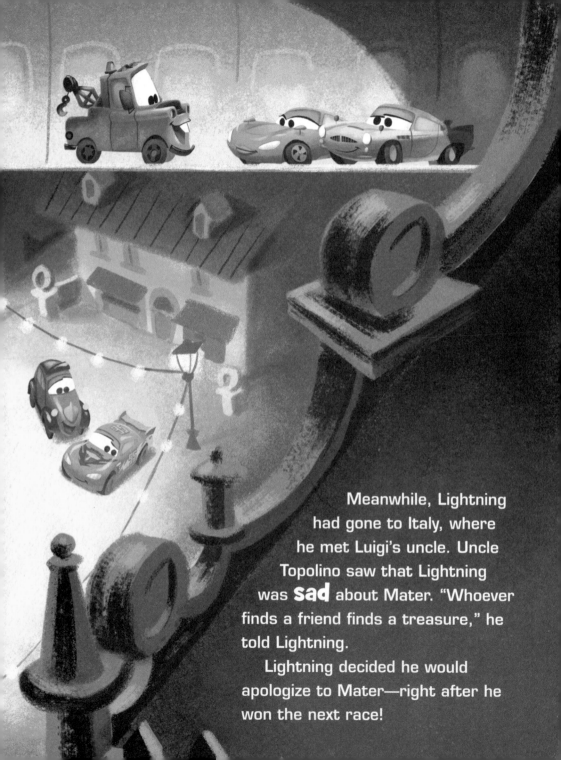

Meanwhile, Lightning had gone to Italy, where he met Luigi's uncle. Uncle Topolino saw that Lightning was **sad** about Mater. "Whoever finds a friend finds a treasure," he told Lightning.

Lightning decided he would apologize to Mater—right after he won the next race!

The next day was the Italy race. Lightning, Francesco, and the other race cars chased each other through the winding streets of Porto Corsa.

Suddenly . . .

BLAM!

KABAM!

Another car
exploded and was
out of the race!

Lightning won! But all the race cars were worried. What was causing them to **explode**?

Mater learned from his new spy friends that Lightning was in danger. But before he could warn his best buddy, the bad cars came back . . .

. . . and **captured** Mater!

Holley and Finn were taken prisoner, too.

The bad guys put the trio in a deadly trap, deep inside **Big Bentley**, the huge London clock!

It was time for the third and final race—in **London**. Once and for all, Lightning and Francesco would find out who was the fastest car in the world.

Suddenly, Mater appeared on the racetrack! He had escaped from the clock! Lightning raced toward Mater to **apologize**. He knew now that winning the race wasn't worth losing his best friend.

But now Mater was driving *away* from Lightning.
He had just realized that the bad guys had planted
a **bomb** . . . right under his hood!

Mater had to get out of
there before it exploded and
hurt Lightning!
But Lightning chased Mater
through the streets of London.

He grabbed on to Mater's hook so his friend couldn't get away.

Then Mater activated his new spy gadgets and took Lightning on a **WILD** ride!

At the last second, Mater figured out how to deactivate the bomb. All the race cars were **saved**!

Mater got a medal from the Queen of England! The rusty old tow truck was a world-class **hero**.

Back in Radiator Springs,
Lightning was happy to be with
all his friends again—especially Mater.
He realized that being the fastest car
in the world wasn't as important
as being a good **friend**.

But Lightning still couldn't pass up a
good race now and then. **VROOM**!